Royal Rescues

The Runaway Rabbit

Paula Harrison

illustrated by Olivia Chin Mueller

Feiwel and Friends • New York

For Emmie, who loves rabbits

A Feiwel and Friends Book
An imprint of Macmillan Publishing Group, LLC
120 Broadway, New York, NY 10271

mackids.com

Our books may be purchased in bulk for promotional, educational,
or business use. Please contact your local bookseller or the Macmillan
Corporate and Premium Sales Department at (800) 221-7945 ext. 5442
or by email at MacmillanSpecialMarkets@macmillan.com.

Library of Congress Cataloging-in-Publication Data is available.

First US edition, 2021
First published in the UK by Nosy Crow
as *Princess of Pets: The Runaway Rabbit* in 2021.

Book design by Nosy Crow and Trisha Previte
Feiwel and Friends logo designed by Filomena Tuosto

Printed in the United States by LSC Communications, Crawfordsville, Indiana

ISBN 978-1-250-79927-2 (hardcover)
1 3 5 7 9 10 8 6 4 2

ISBN 978-1-250-25933-2 (paperback)
1 3 5 7 9 10 8 6 4 2

Chapter One
A Royal Sleepover

Princess Bea raced along the beach, waving a stick over her head. "Here you are, Rosie. Fetch!" She threw the stick into the ocean.

Rosie, a small gray-and-white puppy, leapt into the waves with her tail wagging. Bea laughed as the little dog splashed water everywhere, and Keira, Bea's best friend, giggled, too.

It was a beautiful day, bright and

sunny with a brisk sea breeze. The wispy clouds scudding across the sky mirrored the white-flecked waves below. Rosie galloped out of the sea and dropped the stick at the girls' feet, so Keira picked it up and threw it for her again.

Keira lived at the Sleepy Gull Café with her mom and dad. The café was only a short walk along the clifftop from Ruby Palace, where Bea lived with her brother and sister, and her father, King George. Bea and Keira had brought Rosie to the beach for some exercise. This morning the puppy had gotten very excited and jumped all around the café, so Keira's mom had sent them away with strict instructions to tire the little dog out!

Bea was animal-mad and loved spending time with Rosie, who she'd rescued as a lost puppy last summer. Bea longed for a proper pet of her own, but King George had always told her that keeping animals at the palace was impossible. An animal might knock over a priceless vase or run wild just as an important guest came to visit.

Without a pet of her own, Bea spent her time helping lost or homeless animals instead. She'd already rescued a kitten called Tiger, who lived in the palace kitchens, and helped some ponies that lived at the local farm. Sometimes she and Keira would go riding on Sandy and Bunty, the beautiful dapple-gray ponies, before brushing their manes and giving them peppermint treats!

Keira linked arms with Bea as they walked along the shoreline. "I'm so excited about our sleepover tonight!" she said for the fiftieth time that morning. "I've never slept in a palace before."

Bea grinned. "I can't wait! It's going to be brilliant. I only wish you could bring Rosie, too!"

Rosie, who had returned with the

stick, wagged her tail and gave a soft woof.

"What are we having for dinner? Is it something really fancy?" asked Keira.

"I think it's just spaghetti Bolognese," Bea told her. "But I persuaded Chef Darou to make chocolate brownies for dessert. I know they're your favorite."

"Thanks!" Keira's eyes shone. "And we have to remember to buy sweets and popcorn so we can have a midnight feast!"

"Let's go to the corner shop right now." Bea whistled for Rosie and the puppy came bounding up, shaking the water off her coat.

Keira fastened Rosie's leash to her collar and the girls left the beach, passing a row of waving palm trees as they followed the road into Savara. The main street was busy, and the girls waved to Mr. Patel as they walked past the bakery.

"The best thing is that Mrs. Stickler's away, so there's no one to search my room for sweets and tell us to go to bed early." Bea made a face. Mrs. Stickler was the royal housekeeper, and she had very strict ideas about what was allowed at the palace. "And Dad won't hear us talking because he snores so loudly!"

Keira giggled. "Which sweets shall we buy? Or shall we have chocolate?"

"Let's get both." Bea sped up as they reached the corner shop. "Look, they've got those rainbow gummy stars. I love those!"

Keira quickly brushed the sand off Rosie's coat and followed Bea into the shop. Mrs. Rinberg, the shop owner, smiled at them from behind the counter.

"Morning, Princess Beatrice. Morning, Keira. What are you up to today?"

"I'm going for a sleepover at the palace!" Keira beamed.

"How exciting!" Mrs. Rinberg smiled as she peered at them over the top of her glasses.

"We're having a midnight feast," explained Bea. "So we'll need two packs of these." She picked up the rainbow star sweets.

"And some chocolate, too!" Keira chose a large chocolate bar in a golden wrapper and laid it on the counter.

Soon they had a bag filled with sweets and popcorn—along with a treat for Rosie—and Mrs. Rinberg rang up the total on the till.

"Do you think we've got enough

treats, Rosie?" Bea leaned down to scratch the puppy behind her ears.

Rosie barked loudly and the girls laughed. "Rosie says we *definitely* have enough!" said Keira.

They thanked Mrs. Rinberg and

said goodbye before heading out of the shop. Just as they reached the entrance, the door burst open and a boy rushed in, nearly knocking them over. He had wild hair and mud on his jeans, and he was frowning deeply.

"Watch out!" he growled, running up the newspaper aisle.

"Hey, careful! You nearly stepped on Rosie," Bea told him indignantly.

The boy didn't reply. He rubbed his messy hair, his eyes flicking around the shop. Then he rushed back out the door again.

"That was rude!" Bea glared at the boy as he disappeared around the corner.

"I didn't recognize him," replied Keira. "I wonder who he is."

"If he can't be any nicer, I'm not sure I want to know." Bea took Rosie's leash as they walked down the pavement. The breeze grew stronger, ruffling her hair.

Rosie barked, straining at her leash, and Bea had to grip it tightly to stop her from running into a bush.

"It's all right, Rosie. That boy's

gone now," said Keira soothingly.

Bea caught a strange flicker of movement behind the bush. Was that the wind moving the leaves? She looked a bit closer. Something moved again and a pair of long golden ears popped up.

Rosie whined and pulled even harder on her leash.

"I don't think Rosie's barking about the boy," said Bea. "I think she's seen something. Look, Keira—there's an animal in there!"

"What is it?" Keira tiptoed closer, but Rosie started barking again and the creature dived into the middle of the bush. The leaves quivered as it hid itself among the thickest branches.

"Stop it, Rosie. You're frightening the poor thing!" said Bea.

Keira took the puppy's leash. "Here—I'll take her while you have a look."

Keira pulled Rosie farther away while Bea knelt down and peered through the branches. Among the deep-green leaves there was a pair of brown rabbit eyes looking back at her. She reached out and let the bunny sniff her fingers. The rabbit's nose twitched, and it stared at Bea shyly.

"Hello, little rabbit!" Bea said softly.

"What are you doing in there?"

The bunny edged closer and Bea caught her breath. The animal had a beautiful golden coat with a white tummy and long velvety ears. Bea was sure, from the way the rabbit had sniffed her fingers, that it couldn't be a wild animal. It was much too tame! But what was a pet rabbit doing in the middle of the busiest street in Savara?

Chapter Two
What Rabbits Love Best

Bea reached for the rabbit, hoping to lure it out of the bush, but a truck roared past and the bunny dived back into the undergrowth again. Bea straightened up. "It's a little rabbit with beautiful golden fur," she told Keira. "I'm sure it isn't a wild animal! It's not frightened of me at all. It's just scared of all the loud noises on the street."

Keira nodded, keeping a tight hold

on Rosie's leash. "Do you think it escaped from somewhere?"

"I don't know. Maybe we should ask someone." Bea looked around the busy street. "Excuse me!" She stopped Mr. Tillings from the fishmonger's. "Do you know if anyone's missing a rabbit?"

Mr. Tillings looked surprised. "No, I don't think so! Sorry, Princess Bea—I'm in a terrible hurry with this delivery."

They stopped Mrs. James, the dentist, and then Mr. Owusu, who worked in the harbor office, but neither of them had heard of anyone looking for a rabbit. Between them, Bea and Keira stopped a dozen people, but no one knew anything about a lost bunny. Everyone seemed really busy, and no one offered to stop and help.

"What shall we do?" asked Keira.

"We can't just leave the poor thing under that bush."

Bea wrinkled her forehead. "Maybe there's a way to coax it out." She glanced at Rosie, who was sniffing the shopping bag with her treats inside. "I know! All we need is something that rabbits love to eat."

Racing back into the corner shop, she hurried to the vegetable aisle. There were rows of ripe red tomatoes and deep-purple eggplants, and there were peppers in red, green, and yellow. Bea stared at the huge array of vegetables. She knew rabbits liked green leafy veggies the best, so she gathered up some kale and broccoli.

"It's good to see you girls eating healthy things as well as all those sweets," said Mrs. Rinberg approvingly when

Bea brought the veggies to the counter.

Bea didn't have time to explain. "Thank you very much!" she cried, before running out of the shop again. Then she crouched beside the bush, and pulling some leaves off the bunch of kale, she held them out for the rabbit.

The bunny's nose twitched. Then it hopped a bit closer.

"Come on, little rabbit!" said Bea softly. "I bet you'll love this."

The rabbit hesitated before pushing its nose out of the branches.

"That's it, Bea! I think it's coming out," whispered Keira.

The bunny hopped a little farther. Then it bit off a chunk of kale and chewed it eagerly. Bea stayed as still as possible, letting the rabbit take another bite. Then she moved backward very slowly, letting the creature follow her. Once the rabbit was out of the bush, she would be able to scoop it up safely.

The rabbit chewed the rest of the kale and looked around for more. Keira quickly handed Bea the broccoli. Bea edged back a little more so the rabbit had to come out of hiding to reach the food. The bunny's ears pricked up and it twitched its nose, before hopping a little closer.

Bea waited till the rabbit took a nibble of broccoli, before leaning forward and putting one hand under its furry white tummy. She lifted the bunny into her arms and hugged it tightly. The rabbit's fur felt soft and warm against her cheek. "What shall we call you?" she asked, stroking the rabbit's velvety ears.

"We should call her Goldie because

of her beautiful fur," suggested Keira.

"Goldie suits her!" said Bea, smiling.

Goldie snuggled in Bea's arms, looking very comfortable, until Rosie—who was tired of waiting on the pavement—burst out in a torrent of barking. The rabbit shrank against Bea's chest, her eyes wide.

"Shh, Rosie!" cried Bea. "You're scaring the rabbit."

But the puppy didn't understand. She pulled on her leash, jumping up with her paws on Bea's legs. Goldie started to wriggle out of Bea's grasp.

"It's all right. You're safe with me!" Bea desperately tried to calm her down, but the bunny flexed her strong back legs and sprang right out of Bea's arms.

Goldie landed on the pavement, her ears pricked up in fright. Farther down the road, a cyclist rang his bell. Then a car hooted at the traffic lights. Goldie ran back and forth, jumping at each noise. Bea rushed after the little rabbit, but she slipped out of her reach all over again.

A man came past wheeling a little boy in a stroller. The child gave a shriek as they passed, and Goldie leapt into the air in shock. She swerved away from the stroller and fled down the path, heading straight for the busy road.

"Stop!" Bea gave chase, her heart thumping like a drum.

Keira pulled back on Rosie's leash and held tight, her hand over her mouth.

Goldie went on hopping toward the traffic. A car roared by, sending an empty chip bag swirling into the air. The bunny ran right to the edge of the curb. Her ears were pinned back in terror.

Bea made a grab for the little rabbit, worried she might scare her into leaping across the road. Reaching her just in time, she scooped

Goldie up and pressed her face against the rabbit's fur, her heart still racing. The rabbit burrowed into her

arms, hiding her nose beneath Bea's elbow.

Bea stroked her really gently until she stopped trembling. "That was close!" she told Keira breathlessly. "I thought she was going to run into the road."

"That was *really* close!" agreed Keira. "What are we going to do? We can't just leave her here."

Bea scratched Goldie's ears. "We'll have to take her home with us until we figure out where she came from. Do you think your parents would have her at the café?"

Keira made a face. "I'd love to take her . . . but what about Rosie? She's frightened the bunny twice already!"

"You're right!" Bea stroked Goldie thoughtfully. She wasn't supposed to bring animals back to the palace—

she'd been told that lots of times—but this was an emergency!

Perhaps if she kept her in the garden, then it wouldn't be so bad . . . "I'll take her home then!" She kissed the rabbit's nose. "I think you'll like it at the palace, Goldie!"

Chapter Three

Goldie's New Home

Keira kept Rosie close so the puppy didn't leap up again. "What if someone comes looking for the rabbit after we've gone?"

Bea wrinkled her forehead. "I know! We can ask Mrs. Rinberg to put a note in her window. Lots of people come to the corner shop, so there's a good chance Goldie's owner will see it. Then at least they'll know where the rabbit is."

"That's a brilliant idea! I'll go and ask." Keira took Rosie into the corner shop and came out a minute later, smiling. "Mrs. Rinberg says that's fine! She was busy with lots of customers, but she said she'll put the note in the window as soon as things are quieter."

Bea sighed with relief. "Thanks! Well, I'd better get back to the palace."

"You'd better take these then." Keira handed her friend the shopping bag with the sweets and the popcorn.

"Wow, we've been so busy that I'd almost forgotten about our sleepover!" Bea grinned. "I'm going to make a little house for Goldie in the garden. I'll show it to you when you come over later." She pulled Rosie's dog treat out of the bag. "You'd better take this, though. Rosie might want it."

Rosie gave a loud woof and Keira laughed. "Okay, see you soon!"

The girls said goodbye and Keira headed toward the café. Bea held Goldie tightly as she climbed the hill toward Ruby Palace. Sunshine poured down and the breeze lifted her dark curls.

People smiled and waved, as if they weren't surprised at all to see her with an animal in her arms. The little rabbit settled down, quite happy to be carried all the way up the slope.

By the time Bea reached the palace garden, her arms were starting to ache. She hurried across the grass, hoping she might find Mrs. Cherry by the vegetable plot. The royal gardener was digging the soil next to a row of bean plants. She straightened as Bea came closer and leaned on her garden fork. "Hello, Princess Bea. Who's this you've brought home?"

"This is Goldie!" Bea held out the rabbit to give Mrs. Cherry a closer look.

"Keira and I found her hiding under a bush by the corner shop."

"That's a strange place to find a rabbit! She's beautiful, isn't she?" The gardener tickled Goldie under the chin.

Bea held Goldie tighter as the bunny started to wriggle. "Could you help me figure out somewhere to keep her for now? I know Dad won't like it if I take her to my room."

"Of course! That's very sensible." Mrs. Cherry pushed her fork into the earth before walking to the shed. "Let's see . . . I have a spare wooden crate that held last year's strawberries. If we tie an empty sack over the top as a roof, that would make quite a good hutch for a day or two."

Bea set Goldie down inside an empty wheelbarrow and helped the gardener fasten the sack onto the corners of the crate. The pen had narrow gaps between each slat so that air and light could get inside.

"We'd better see if Goldie likes it!" Bea turned around to find that the rabbit had jumped out of the wheelbarrow and hopped across the vegetable plot. The bunny stopped beside a patch of carrots and began nibbling at the greens.

"Well, at least she's found something nice to eat," said Mrs. Cherry, smiling. "Now, let's move this makeshift hutch into one corner so that my wheelbarrow and other things will fit inside the shed, too."

Bea and the gardener had just finished moving things around the shed, when they heard a loud gasp. Mr. Darou, the palace chef, was hurrying toward them with a horrified look on his face. "Get off, you horrible creature!" He flapped his white chef's hat at the bunny. "Get away from those carrots."

"It's all right!" called Mrs. Cherry. "Princess Bea rescued the little rabbit and we're just setting up somewhere to keep her."

Darou took no notice. "Look at that—it's nibbled every single one. Shoo, you nasty thing!" Flapping his hat in the air, he dashed across the vegetable plot and trampled some of the bean shoots.

Goldie pricked up her ears and quickly hopped away. Hiding behind a row of tomato plants, she peeked out timidly.

Bea hurried out of the shed. She wished the chef would stop shouting and flapping his hat around. "It's all right—I'll catch her. She's quite a nervous rabbit, so if you keep on doing that, she might run off."

"This is terrible!" Darou stormed. "I *promised* the king I would make carrot soup for dinner, as it's his favorite. Now that *creature* has spoiled everything!"

"I have some lovely leeks and potatoes that would make a nice soup," offered Mrs. Cherry, but the chef only grew crosser.

"I simply *cannot* cook with animals galloping around and chewing everything!" He kicked out at the vegetable plot, sending clods of earth flying into the air.

A large lump of soil landed right next to Goldie. The rabbit jumped in fright, her little white tail flashing as she ran to the edge of the vegetable garden. She squeezed under the wire fence and made off across the palace lawn.

Mrs. Cherry put a hand on Bea's arm, murmuring, "You go and catch her, Princess Bea. I'll calm Mr. Darou down and see if I can send him back to the kitchen."

Bea raced after the little bunny. Goldie dived into the middle of some lilies and hid there, camouflaged among

the bright yellow and white flowers. Bea spotted the tall lily stems quivering.

"I'm sorry, Goldie!" She knelt down on the grass and held out her hand. "I know Chef Darou seems scary, but I can keep you safe if you trust me."

Goldie sniffed her fingers, just like she had when Bea had discovered her in the bush.

"Come and try the new hutch we've made for you," Bea continued. "You must be so tired after all this running around."

Goldie eyed her cautiously. Then she hopped out of her hiding place and twitched her nose. Bea smiled as she stroked the rabbit's soft ears. Goldie must really trust her to come out of hiding so quickly!

"Everything will be fine, you'll see!" Bea lifted the rabbit into her arms. "I'll make your hutch really comfortable and bring you some lovely things to eat." She carried Goldie back to the shed. Luckily, there was no sign of the royal chef.

Bea gently put Goldie inside the homemade hutch and laid some straw across the bottom. Then she left a saucer of water for the bunny to drink

and fastened the last corner of the roof sacking. Finally, she pushed a few leafy carrot tops through the gaps in the wooden slats. "Although I expect you're quite full now—after all the things you've eaten!" she told the rabbit.

Goldie twitched her nose and scampered up and down. Bea sighed with relief. The little rabbit was safe at last. She crouched down beside the crate and watched Goldie for a while. The bunny nibbled a carrot top before lying down on the straw.

Bea jumped up and dusted off her hands. Goldie seemed really happy in her hutch, and now Bea had a special sleepover to get ready for!

Chapter Four
The Bunny Muddle

Keira arrived at five o'clock carrying a bag with her pajamas, a toothbrush, and Gruff, her favorite teddy, inside. Bea met her at the door and they raced upstairs together, giggling.

"I put up the air mattress for you—it's quite comfy!" Bea bounced up and down to show Keira how squashy it was.

"Thanks, Bea! Did you hide the sweets somewhere?" asked Keira excitedly.

"Yes, don't worry!" Bea told her. "I couldn't leave them lying about with Alfie around. Do you want to come and see Goldie?"

"Yes, please!" cried Keira.

They rushed back downstairs and raced across the palace garden to the shed. Bea proudly showed Keira the hutch. "Mrs. Cherry helped me put this together. See—Goldie's got everything she needs."

"I think it looks brilliant!" Keira knelt beside the little hutch. "Hello, Goldie! How are you?"

The rabbit nibbled contentedly on some carrot leaves. Then she hopped across the hay and took a drink of water. Her coat was soft and golden except inside her ears, where there were little tufts of white fur.

Footsteps sounded outside the shed and Bea's little brother, Alfie, appeared in the doorway. "What are you doing? I heard you say something about sweets."

"Alfie, stop snooping! This is nothing to do with you," cried Bea.

"Ooh, what's that? Why are you keeping a rabbit in here? Can I feed it?" asked Alfie.

"No, you can't!" said Bea. "Keira and I found her, so we're the ones looking after her."

"That's not fair!" Her brother turned bright red. "Why do *you* get to do anything you like? I'm telling Dad!" He ran off across the lawn.

"Maybe we should have let him help a bit," suggested Keira.

Bea sighed. "I'll let him help tomorrow. Shall we get Goldie out of the hutch for a while?"

The girls lifted the rabbit out of the pen and took turns stroking her. Bea was just about to return the little rabbit to the shed when King George came striding across the lawn.

"Beatrice, where did you get that rabbit from?" he said sternly. "Please tell me you haven't brought a wild animal home."

Bea explained that they'd found Goldie near the corner shop and that Mrs. Rinberg had put a sign in the shop window asking if anyone had lost a pet rabbit. Then she showed her father Goldie's homemade hutch.

"I know it's not as good as a proper hutch, but I think Goldie will be happy here for a few days," she added.

Keira brought the bunny closer and the king's face softened as he patted Goldie's fur. "I think you've been very sensible about this, girls. When Alfred came to me with a tale about a rabbit

on the loose, I expected the worst, but I think a temporary hutch in the garden is an excellent idea . . . and you've already taken steps to find the animal's owner, too."

Bea smiled widely. "Thanks, Dad! She's such a sweet rabbit. I really couldn't leave her all alone in Savara."

"Yes, well . . . Obviously it would be too much to ask you not to bring animals back to the palace altogether!" King George raised his eyebrows at Bea.

"We could run down the hill and see if anyone's asked Mrs. Rinberg about Goldie," Keira said. "You never know, Bea—someone might have seen the note in the window already!"

"That's a good idea!" said Bea. "Is that all right, Dad?"

The king nodded. "Just make sure you're back in time for dinner."

Bea and Keira hurried out of the palace gate. The breeze ruffled their hair as they raced down the hill. They slowed down as they reached the row of shops beside the harbor. The street was quieter than it had been that morning. The sun had turned a beautiful burnt orange as it sank toward the sea.

"There's the notice!" Bea pointed to a piece of paper stuck on the window of the corner shop. It read *LOST RABBIT* in big capital letters. "Let's find out if anyone's asked about Goldie."

"Bea, wait!" Keira grabbed her friend's arm. "Look at the rest of the note."

Bea hastily scanned what Mrs. Rinberg had written. Something halfway down caught her eye . . . *so if you are missing a toy rabbit with golden fur, come and speak to me to find out who is looking after him.*

Bea sucked in her breath. "A TOY rabbit! But Goldie isn't a toy."

"There's been a mix-up." Keira made a face. "I'm sure I told Mrs. Rinberg that Goldie was a real rabbit, but she was busy with a whole line of customers, so maybe she didn't listen very carefully."

"But if Goldie's owner comes by, they won't know the sign is about their pet. We have to tell her about the mistake right now!" Bea burst through the shop door. "Mrs. Rinberg, are you there?"

"Hello, my dear." Mrs. Rinberg looked up from her till. "Have you come for more sweets? Surely you haven't eaten the other ones already?"

"No, it's about the sign in the window," Bea said quickly. "The rabbit we found on the path outside was a real one—not a toy."

Mrs. Rinberg looked at them over the top of her glasses. "Oh, really! I thought it was a furry toy. Wasn't that what you told me?"

Keira shook her head. "She's a real rabbit! We think she must be someone's pet."

The door banged and the boy they'd run into that morning came in. Bea frowned, remembering how rude he'd been before. She turned back to the shopkeeper. "Could I change the sign so that it says a *real* rabbit? Then you can tell anyone who asks that she's safe and sound at the palace. I'm keeping her in a hutch in the garden shed."

"Of course, dear!" Mrs. Rinberg handed her a pen. "I think it's wonderful that you're looking after the creature. Mr. Patel was saying only the other day what an animal lover you are."

Bea pulled the sign down from the window and crossed out the word *toy*. In the space above it she wrote the word *pet* instead. She gave the pen back to Mrs. Rinberg, nearly colliding with the grumpy-looking boy, who was fidgeting next to the baked beans. Why was he staring at her like that?

"Excuse me!" The boy scowled deeply.

"I don't know if I'm supposed to bow or something but—"

Bea glared back. "Don't bother! We don't want to get in your way again." Pulling Keira after her, she hurried out of the shop and the door closed behind them. "That boy is so annoying!" she said.

"I know—just ignore him! At least the sign says the right thing now." Keira smoothed her hair back. "Let's go back to Ruby Palace. Then after dinner we can get into our pajamas and watch a movie."

Bea smiled back. "And then we can have our midnight feast!"

Chapter Five

A Mystery at Midnight

After they said good night to Goldie, Bea and Keira changed into their pajamas. They watched their favorite movie, *Rusty the Amazing Detective Dog*, before going back to Bea's room to share the sweets.

"What shall we start with? Chocolate or rainbow stars?" said Bea, taking the sweets from the bottom of her wardrobe where she'd been hiding them.

"Chocolate!" Keira looked around suddenly. "Did you hear that?"

Bea heard a soft creak in the hall outside. She crept to the door, opening it quickly to reveal Alfie standing there. "Alfie! What are you doing? This isn't your sleepover."

"But you've got sweets." Alfie's eyes lit up.

"Why would I give you any? You told on me to Dad!" Bea said sternly.

Alfie made a face. "I only said there was a rabbit in the shed. I didn't think it was a secret. You can't eat all that stuff by yourselves. It's not fair!"

Bea opened one of the packets of rainbow stars and poured a few sweets into her brother's hands. "Now, go away or *I'll* tell Dad!"

Alfie slunk off down the corridor. Bea

and Keira snuggled down under the blankets to share the chocolate.

"I wonder who Goldie's owner is," said Keira.

"They must be really missing her," said Bea. "She's such an adorable rabbit."

The girls finished the chocolate and ate half the rainbow sweets. At last they turned the lights off and Bea opened the curtains a little so she could see the stars appearing one by one in the sky. She lay back in bed watching the full moon shining through the window. She hoped Goldie was comfortable in her homemade hutch in the garden shed. She couldn't wait till tomorrow morning when she could play with the little rabbit again!

Something woke Bea suddenly. The room was dark. Keira was lying on the air mattress, fast asleep with the blanket pulled up to her chin. An empty chocolate wrapper lay on the floor nearby. Bea glanced through the gap in the curtains, wondering what had woken her. A cloud was passing in front of the moon, and the garden was completely black, except for one patch of light in the middle.

Bea climbed out of bed and opened the curtains more. The light was moving. It had to be someone with a flashlight. Bea checked her alarm clock. It was nearly midnight. Why was someone shining a flashlight around the garden in the middle of the night?

She leaned closer to the glass. The flashlight beam stopped moving and shone straight at the royal vegetable plot. The rows of tomatoes and beans

suddenly stood out in the light. Bea held her breath, watching closely, but she couldn't see who was holding the light.

Tiptoeing across the room, she tapped Keira on the shoulder. "Hey! There's someone out in the garden. Come and see!"

Keira turned over, mumbling, "Go back to sleep, Bea! It's too early to get up."

"I know—it's midnight!" said Bea. "But someone's out there with a flashlight and I don't know why."

Keira propped herself up on one elbow and rubbed her eyes. "Someone's out where?"

"In the garden! I can see them shining a light around." Bea returned to the window and peered out. "Actually, they're still looking at the vegetable plot. I hope it's not a burglar!"

"Why would a burglar steal vegetables?" Keira joined Bea at the window, yawning.

Bea caught a glimpse of a shadowy figure behind the light as it moved. She bit her lip. "Maybe it's a ghost!"

Keira nudged her friend. "Ghosts don't carry flashlights! Maybe it's Alfie trying to play with Goldie while we're asleep, or maybe Mrs. Cherry is looking for the slugs and snails that eat her vegetables."

Bea frowned. Alfie was definitely capable of going out in the middle of the night to look at the rabbit, but he had seemed more interested in their sweets than Goldie.

Suddenly the beam of light vanished.

Then it reappeared, and this time it was wobbling wildly. It pointed at the sky, at the ground, and everywhere in between, as if it was doing a crazy dance.

Keira shivered. "I don't like this! Maybe we should tell someone . . ."

"Maybe we should find out what's going on first. If it's Alfie, I don't want to get him into trouble." Bea thought quickly. "I know! Come with me." She put on her slippers and tiptoed down the hallway, with Keira following.

Halfway along the passage, she stopped by Alfie's room and pressed her ear to the door. There was no sound. Bea carefully turned the handle and opened the door a little.

Alfie was lying in bed with his eyes shut and his mouth wide open. For a second, Bea wanted to giggle. Then she

caught sight of Keira's worried face. If it wasn't Alfie in the garden, then who was it?

She ran down the corridor and dashed into her dad's room. "Dad, wake up! There's someone in the garden."

Her father went on snoring gently. He was in stripy pajamas, and his crown

was hanging off the bedpost. Bea tapped him on the shoulder before trying again. "There's someone with a flashlight on the palace grounds. We can't tell who it is! I think you should come and look."

King George mumbled something

and turned over before going back to sleep.

"Sometimes it's really hard to wake him," Bea explained to Keira. "I think we should find out who it is on our own."

They tiptoed down the hallway and peered out of the window at the top of the stairs. The flashlight had stopped moving again. Darkness lay thickly over the garden except for one beam of light.

Keira gasped. "It's pointing right at the shed."

Bea's heart sank. Keira was right. The beam was shining straight at the garden shed where Goldie was sleeping. Did the owner of the flashlight know there was an animal inside? Was the little rabbit in danger?

"I'm going out there!" she told

Keira. "I have to make sure Goldie's safe."

Keira swallowed, her voice trembling. "Then I'm coming with you!"

Chapter Six

Whispers in the Dark

Bea raced down the palace stairs, nearly missing the last step in the dark. Keira hurried after her and bumped into Bea at the bottom.

"Sorry!" Keira grabbed the stair rail to keep her balance. "Hold on, Bea! We can't rush out there in our pajamas."

"Here—we'll put these over our night things." Bea pulled two jackets from the coat rack and then handed her friend some shoes. "You'd better put these on, too."

They dashed into the royal kitchen, and Bea searched the drawers for a flashlight. The pots and pans hanging on the walls gleamed in the faint light coming through the windows. Tiger, the little palace cat, ran out of the laundry room where he slept. He mewed and rubbed against their legs as if he wanted attention.

"What's the matter, Tiger?" said Bea. "You can't be hungry."

The kitten went on mewing and weaving around their feet.

Bea stroked his stripy orange fur. "I'll give you extra cuddles tomorrow, I promise," she told the cat. "But right now there's something I've got to do."

Tiger gave a shrill meow and swiped at Bea's leg with his little claws.

"Ow!" she cried. "That wasn't very nice! What's got into you?"

Tiger gave her a fierce look and ran over to the laundry room and back again, mewing loudly.

But Bea was rummaging in the back

of a kitchen drawer and ignored the little kitten. She pulled out a flashlight, jumping in fright as the refrigerator whirred. Then she took a deep breath to slow her racing heartbeat. "I'll test this light just in case, but I won't keep it on yet," she said to Keira. "We don't want whoever's out there to see us!"

The darkness folded around them as they stepped outside. Strange little sounds filled the royal garden. Something rustled in the undergrowth, and fallen leaves swooshed along the ground in the breeze. Tree branches swayed, sending spiny shadows dancing across the palace lawn.

Keira shivered and linked arms with Bea. "It's spooky out here! Are you sure this is a good idea?"

"We need to find out who's shining

that light at the shed," Bea whispered back. "Don't worry—I know this garden so well I can find loads of places for us to hide."

They crept across the garden, staying close to hedges and fountains and anything else large enough to hide behind. Bea paused at each hiding place, checking that it was safe to move on.

The flashlight beam on the other side of the garden began to move again, jiggling to and fro as if whoever held the flashlight was moving over rough ground.

The full moon appeared from behind a cloud just as Bea and Keira made a nerve-racking dash across the palace driveway. Luckily, the moonlight vanished again a moment later and the girls trod lightly, hoping the gravel wouldn't crunch under their feet. They hid behind a bush close to the palace wall and watched the beam wobbling overhead.

"The light seems really high up," whispered Keira. "Do you think they've climbed on top of the wall?"

"Maybe!" Bea peered through the darkness. "No . . . look! They're in the tree on the other side. That's why the light's

moving—the tree's swaying in the wind."

The beam suddenly swung in their direction, and the girls ducked and hid their faces. A moment later, the beam of light shifted back to the garden shed.

"Do you think they heard us?" Keira murmured into Bea's ear.

"I don't know. I wish I could see who it is," Bea hissed back. She squinted as hard as she could. Now and then, as the flashlight moved, she caught a glimpse of an arm or a shoulder. But most of the time the figure was hidden behind the beam.

"I'm going to switch on my flashlight for a second," Bea whispered. "If I shine the beam just above theirs it should light up their face."

"All right then," Keira said faintly. "I'm ready to run if we have to."

Bea pointed the flashlight carefully, her finger on the button. "Five . . . four . . . three . . . two . . . one . . ." She flicked the switch, sending a beam of light over the palace wall.

Instantly, the tree beyond the wall was lit up in the beam. The branches stuck out like fingers, and Bea glimpsed a boy's face among the leaves. His eyes widened in shock and he shielded his face from the bright light.

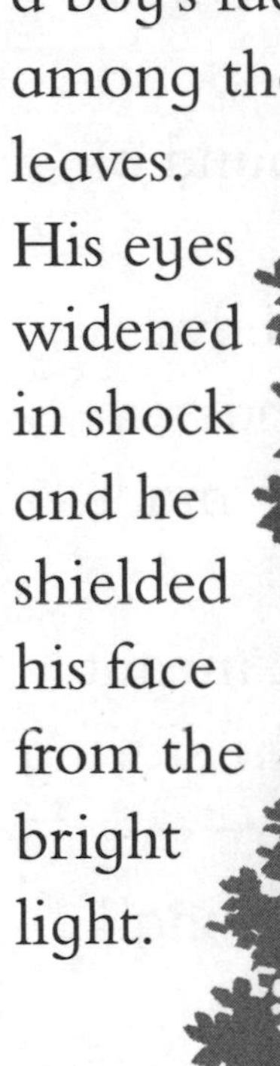

"It's that boy from the shop!" Keira gasped.

Bea froze, her light fixed on the boy's face. What on earth was he doing here?

The boy tried to shade his eyes. He fumbled for his flashlight, but it slipped out of his fingers. He made a grab for it, swaying wildly. Then he lost his balance and tumbled out of the tree, disappearing behind the wall.

There was a yell and the sound of branches cracking.

Bea winced. The boy must have fallen all the way to the ground.

"Oh no!" Keira gulped. "We made him fall. It's all our fault!"

Bea's heart sank. She hadn't meant to hurt anybody. "But why is he staring into our garden in the middle of the night? He must be up to something!"

"He could be injured," said Keira. "We should see if he's all right."

Bea scrambled out of the hiding place and ran her flashlight up and down the tree trunk. The boy didn't reappear. "Are you all right?" she called out. "Did you hurt yourself?"

There was no answer.

"Maybe he ran away," said Keira.

There was a rustling sound from behind the wall. Bea frowned. It sounded like the boy was still there.

Questions whirled around Bea's head. Why had the boy been shining his flashlight into the royal garden? And why had he been so rude in the shop earlier that day? None of it made any sense.

"I'm going over there!" she said to Keira. "I need to make sure he's okay, and anyway I want to know what he's up to."

She marched up to the palace wall and began to climb.

Chapter Seven
The Strange Boy

Bea struggled to find handholds and footholds in the palace wall. Her fingers slipped down the smooth bricks as soon as she began to climb. Keira held the flashlight to light up the wall. "Look, Bea! It gets easier to climb near the top."

"Hold on—I've got an idea!" Bea ran to the palace shed. She pulled out the wheelbarrow and lined it up against the wall.

After climbing into the barrow, she reached for the handholds between each brick and scrambled up the wall. Keira kept the light trained on the bricks to show the way. The bushes on

the other side rustled as Bea hauled herself to the top.

A beam of light flashed on, shining right into her eyes. "Hey!" she called down. "Can you shine that somewhere else?"

"Sorry!" came the boy's reply, and the beam shifted away.

Bea blinked, her eyes adjusting to the dark. She spotted a figure sitting on the ground at the bottom of the wall. He was bent over, rubbing his knee.

"Did you hurt yourself?" she called down, but there was no reply. Bea swung her legs over the top and began climbing down the other side.

The boy scrambled to his feet as she reached the bottom. Bea studied him closely. He was definitely the same boy she'd met in the corner shop—with the wild hair and the scowl.

"Are you hurt?" she asked again. "We called to you when you fell, but you didn't answer."

"I'm fine!" he said grumpily. "You didn't need to climb all the way over here to check on me."

Bea rolled her eyes. He really was the most prickly person she'd ever met. "Me and my friend Keira wanted to make sure you were all right. I'm Bea, by the way."

"I'm Harry," he muttered. "I should probably get back home . . ."

The moon came out from behind a cloud and Bea searched the boy's face. He glanced at her before rubbing his forehead awkwardly. Bea suddenly felt a bit sorry for him. She'd feel embarrassed, too, if she fell out of a tree.

"Don't go yet!" she said. "You haven't told me why you're here. It's the middle of the night!"

Harry shifted from one foot to the other. "I know. Sorry about that—"

"So what *are* you doing here?" Bea interrupted. "You can't go around shining your flashlight into other people's gardens. I could see the light from my bedroom window."

"I wasn't trying to wake anyone!" protested Harry.

"And you were really rude this morning in the shop!" Bea added.

Harry sniffed and blinked quickly. "I know, I'm sorry. I was just worried about my rabbit. I couldn't find her anywhere."

Bea's eyes widened in surprise. "Your rabbit! You mean *you're* the one who lost the bunny?"

Harry nodded. "Trixie's always been good at escaping—she'll squeeze through any little gap at the bottom of her pen—but she's never run right out of the garden before." He sniffed again. "This morning, our neighbors chopped down a tree, and it was so loud that it spooked her. I spent all day looking for her."

Bea sat down on a log at the bottom of the tree. "We found her behind a bush on the main road. We tried to find out who she belonged to, but no one knew, so I brought her back here. She's living in a homemade hutch in my garden shed."

"I know! I heard what you said to the shopkeeper the second time I saw you . . ." Harry twisted his fingers together. "Look—I'm sorry I was rude!"

"Oh, don't worry about that!" Bea said quickly. "But why didn't you stop me when you heard me talking about your rabbit?"

"I tried to but, you wouldn't listen! So

I decided I'd come here and check that Trixie was all right." He hesitated, before sitting down next to Bea on the log.

"Sorry I didn't listen," Bea said sheepishly.

Harry shrugged. "I guess it was mostly my fault. I was just so worried about Trixie."

"We've been calling her Goldie because of her lovely fur," explained Bea. "Our gardener helped me make a little hutch for her, and she's been eating lots of carrot tops."

Harry smiled. "She really likes those! We used to grow our own carrots at our old house, but since we moved to Savara, we haven't had time." He looked at her shyly. "Thanks for looking after her."

"No problem!" Bea jumped up. "Why don't you come and see her right now?

We'll have to climb over because the palace gate's always locked at night."

Suddenly Keira called from the other side of the wall. "Bea, are you okay? You've been gone for ages."

"Everything's all right," Bea called back. "We're climbing over now."

Together she and Harry clambered up the wall. Harry stuck his flashlight into his pocket so he had both hands free. They swung their legs over the top and climbed down the other side, while Keira used her flashlight to light the way.

Bea jumped down and dusted off her hands. "Keira, this is Harry! He's Goldie's owner . . . except Goldie's actually called Trixie."

Keira looked surprised. "Oh! So it was your rabbit all along."

"Yes, she ran away this morning."

Harry smiled shyly. "Sorry I scared you all—shining the light over the wall like that."

"Oh, we weren't really scared!" said Bea, forgetting how nervous she'd felt when they'd sneaked across the garden.

"I was, a little!" said Keira. "But I'm really glad we've found out who Goldie belongs to."

"Come and see the hutch I made her!" Bea grabbed Harry's arm and led him over to the garden shed.

They crouched beside Goldie's hutch and Keira shone the torch gently inside.

"Goldie, are you asleep?" Bea peered through the wooden slats. Was the rabbit hiding underneath the hay?

"She's not in there—look." Keira pointed to a broken corner of the crate. A small piece of wood had been chewed off, leaving a little hole.

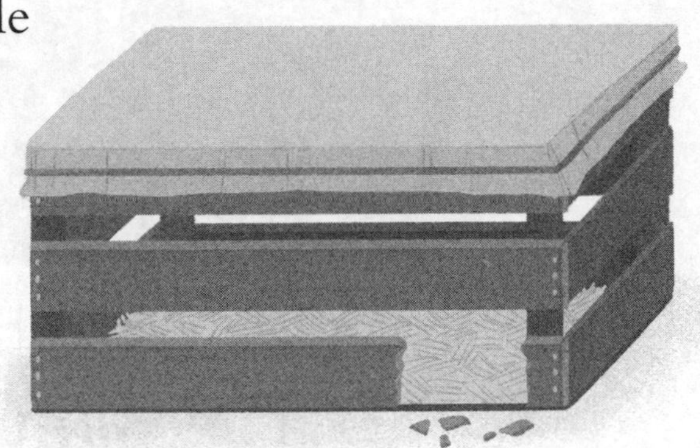

"She's escaped again!" Harry clutched his unruly hair. "How am I going to find her in the dark? She could have gone anywhere."

"We'll look for her together," Bea said firmly. "And we won't stop searching till we've found her!"

Chapter Eight
The Hunt for Goldie

Bea darted out of the shed and flashed her light along the rows of plants. Harry did the same and Keira ran around the vegetable plot, looking everywhere.

"I don't think she's here!" panted Keira.

"But she loves broccoli and beans, and it doesn't look as if she even took a nibble!" Harry stared at the vegetables. "I hope there wasn't a fox here . . ."

Bea's stomach lurched. She hoped nothing awful had happened to Goldie. She shone her light along the wire fence that separated the vegetables from the rest of the palace garden. "There aren't any holes in the fence big enough for a fox, but look!" She pointed to a small gap in the wire. A piece of carrot lay next to the hole. "That has to be how Goldie escaped."

"But where did she go next? Your garden is so huge!" Harry swept his beam in a big circle.

"Don't worry—we'll find her!" Bea called back, as she raced out of the vegetable plot.

She went to the herb garden first, before looking around the orchard. Harry and Keira ran after her and they searched each place thoroughly.

Harry called to his rabbit as he flashed his light under bushes and behind trees. They worked quickly, but the orchard was especially large and took a long time to search.

Harry rubbed his hair. "Trixie could be miles away by now."

"Let's split up to save time," Keira suggested.

"Are you sure you won't get lost?" said Bea doubtfully.

"Harry and I can search over here close to the palace." Keira pointed to the main flower beds. "And you can check the stables and the fountains because you know where you're going."

"Good idea! I won't be long." Bea ran off toward the stables.

The stable yard was strangely still and quiet in the dark. Bea checked each stall in the stable block just in case Goldie had decided she liked the horses' warm hay. Then she checked the fountains before running back to the others. She shook her head. "I couldn't find her."

"What shall we do? We're getting nowhere!" Harry burst out.

"Maybe we should try waking the king again?" said Keira.

"I guess we could—" began Bea.

"No, don't do that!" cried Harry. "I'll get in trouble for sneaking over here, and I don't want to be thrown into your dungeon."

Bea frowned. "We don't have a dungeon! But if we wake my dad, he'll only tell us to look for Goldie in the morning . . ." She chewed her lip worriedly. "I guess we should go back to the vegetable plot and see if we missed any clues. Maybe she left a footprint somewhere."

Bea led them along the path, flashing her light into every possible hiding place. A hollow feeling grew inside her stomach. What if there had been a fox, like Harry said? She was trying to stay cheerful, but it felt as if they'd been searching for hours and there was still no sign of the little rabbit.

They hurried around the corner by the palace kitchen. Then, just as they passed the back door, Bea spotted something in the beam of her flashlight. Lying on the path was a small sprig of carrot leaves.

Bea bent down to pick the leaves up, and her heart skipped. "Look at this! Goldie must have dropped them."

Harry shone his light along the path. "Then where is she?"

"She could be hiding." Keira peered behind some flowerpots.

"Maybe . . ." Bea stared at the carrot leaves and a strange idea popped into her head. "I think she might have gone inside. Chef Darou often leaves the door open when he's cooking. He likes the fresh air."

Harry's mouth dropped open. "You mean . . . she's inside the palace?"

Bea nodded. "Chef was making vegetable soup for dinner. Maybe Goldie liked the smell and she hopped inside." She opened the door to the kitchen and shone her light around.

Harry hesitated before following the girls into the room. He rubbed his cheek nervously. "Are you sure it's all right that I'm here?" he whispered.

"Shh!" said Bea. "I think I heard something!"

Suddenly Tiger sprang out from behind a cupboard with a shrill meow. They all jumped.

"Tiger, what *are* you doing?" said Bea. "We haven't got time to play with you right now."

The little cat ran toward the passageway. Then he stopped and fixed his bright green eyes on them.

"It's like he's trying to tell us something," said Keira.

Bea followed Tiger into the hallway. "What's the matter, Tiger? Where are you taking us?"

Tiger ran across to the laundry room and stopped again. Bea followed the kitten and flicked on the light switch. Curled up in Tiger's basket was Goldie, and next to her were six tiny bundles. All the baby rabbits had

little pink ears and noses. They cuddled against their mother's tummy with their eyes shut tight.

Bea gasped. "Tiger, you're such a clever cat! And look at all the babies!"

"Trixie!" cried Harry. "Are you all right?" He rushed past Bea and then stopped suddenly, staring at the little velvety bundles curled up beside the mother rabbit.

"No wonder Tiger wanted our help," said Keira, smiling. "His basket has been taken over by rabbits. Don't they look cute together!"

Tiger scampered up to his basket and gently sniffed at the bunnies, before backing away a little.

"Did you know she was having babies?" Bea asked Harry.

"No, I had no idea!" Harry

crouched beside the basket and stroked his rabbit gently. "She must have been looking for somewhere soft and warm to have her kits—that's what you call baby rabbits—and this was the best place she could find."

Bea knelt beside him and gazed at the tiny kits. "They're beautiful! And now you'll have seven rabbits instead of one."

"Thanks so much for finding them!" Harry said shyly.

Bea grinned. "I think we should really be saying thank you to Tiger."

"Meow!" said Tiger, waving his stripy tail.

Chapter Nine
New Friends

Harry stroked his rabbit and checked that each of the kits was warm and comfortable. Bea took a laundry basket and padded it with towels so that Tiger had his own bed again.

"I should probably go home," Harry said with a yawn. "It's really late and my mom and dad will be cross if they find I'm out of bed."

"Don't worry, your rabbits will be safe here till the morning," said Bea.

Harry nodded. "If I bring my pet carrier tomorrow, I can take them home."

"Why don't you come for breakfast first?" Bea said quickly. "Then you can have some of Chef's pancakes. They're really yummy!"

"I don't really know if I can stay that long!" Harry avoided her gaze. "I might be busy."

Bea frowned. How could anyone be too busy for pancakes? "Hold on," she said slowly. "Why didn't you come to find your rabbit earlier? You heard us talking in the shop and you could have come here right away. Why did you wait till the middle of the night?"

Harry went red. "It's just. . . I know you're a princess!"

Bea stared at him. "What do you mean?"

"I'm not used to palaces and royalty," he said awkwardly. "I might bow at the wrong time or say the wrong thing!"

Bea burst out laughing. "Sorry!" she gasped. "It's just I'm always saying the wrong thing. But my dad, King George, is always nice to guests, so he won't mind you visiting."

"He's always nice to me!" Keira agreed. "And he's often busy in his royal study anyway."

Harry stroked his rabbit's soft coat. "Well, if you're sure it's okay . . . I do like pancakes."

"Then come first thing tomorrow," Bea said firmly. "And we promise to look after all the rabbits till then."

Harry thanked them and gave his

bunny one more stroke. Bea and Keira helped him find his way back over the palace wall, lighting the way with the flashlight.

"Harry seemed so grumpy when we first met him," Bea said to Keira as they crept back inside. "But he isn't really like that at all—he's just a bit shy, like his rabbit!"

Bea and Keira slept deeply after all the excitement, and when they woke up the next morning, the smell of freshly made pancakes was drifting up the stairs. The girls put on jeans and T-shirts and hurried downstairs, their stomachs rumbling. Natasha, Bea's older sister, and Alfie were already in the dining room, eating breakfast.

"Alfie!" Natasha tried to wrestle

the plate of pancakes from her little brother. "You can't have another one. You've had three already!"

"Well, *they* had loads of sweets last night," Alfie said, nodding at Bea and Keira. "So why can't I have extra pancakes?"

"We've got a guest coming this morning," said Bea, ignoring Alfie. "We found the boy who owns the rabbit and his name is Harry. He's coming soon to collect his pet."

"How did you find him so fast?" Natasha let go of the plate and Alfie picked up two more pancakes. "I thought you had no idea whose rabbit it was."

"It turned out that we'd already met Harry at the corner shop," said Bea, skipping the part where they'd sneaked around the garden at midnight.

"It was good luck, really!" added Keira.

There was a knock at the palace front door.

"That'll be him now!" said Bea.

The girls dashed to the front door and found Harry on the palace steps. He was holding a large pet carrier and shifting nervously from one foot to the other.

"Hello, we're just having breakfast. You said you like pancakes. Come and have some!" Bea pulled him inside and took him to the dining room. "Everyone—this is Harry."

"Hello!" said Alfie between mouthfuls.

Natasha smiled at Harry. "Sorry, there are no pancakes left. I'll get Chef to make some more."

Alfie ran off to play and Natasha headed for the kitchen, returning with a plate of tasty pancakes. She had just handed some to Harry, with some chocolate sauce, when King George marched in.

"Mmm, pancakes! I thought something smelled nice." He stared at Harry for a moment. "Good gracious—who's this?"

Harry went red, so Bea said quickly, "This is Harry—he's come to collect the lost rabbit."

"Really?" The king smiled. "And how did the bunny escape in the first place?"

Harry stammered as he explained that his rabbit was extremely good at running away. The king sat down to listen while helping himself to a pancake. Then he asked Harry lots of questions about keeping a rabbit. When they had finished breakfast, the king nodded to Harry and said, "Very nice to meet you! And good luck with your rabbits."

"He's just like an ordinary dad, isn't he?" said Harry, as they went to the laundry room with the pet carrier. "I thought a king would be scarier than that."

"Now you can come and visit whenever you like," said Bea. "And maybe I could come to your house to see the rabbit babies."

They reached the laundry room. Goldie was cuddled up in Tiger's basket with her six tiny babies. She pricked up her ears as the children came in. Harry knelt beside her and stroked her soft fur. Tiger, who was curled up in his makeshift bed nearby, opened his eyes and mewed.

"You can definitely come and visit us," Harry told Bea. "I might need some help looking after seven rabbits!"

"Maybe your dad will let you adopt one," Keira said to Bea.

"I wondered that, too!" Bea's eyes shone. "Wouldn't it be lovely to have another pet at the palace, Tiger?"

Tiger jumped out of his basket and nuzzled Bea's hand before scampering off to find his breakfast. Bea crouched beside Harry and stroked the bunny's ears. The kits wriggled against their mother's fur, their eyes still shut tight.

"Thanks for looking after them all," said Harry. "You're not really a normal princess, are you?"

"Not really!" Bea grinned. "I'm a princess of pets!"

Thank you for reading this **Feiwel and Friends** book.

The Friends who made

ROYAL RESCUES

The Runaway Rabbit

possible are:

Jean Feiwel, Publisher

Liz Szabla, Associate Publisher

Rich Deas, Senior Creative Director

Holly West, Senior Editor

Anna Roberto, Senior Editor

Kat Brzozowski, Senior Editor

Dawn Ryan, Executive Managing Editor

Kim Waymer, Senior Production Manager

Erin Siu, Associate Editor

Emily Settle, Associate Editor

Foyinsi Adegbonmire, Associate Editor

Rachel Diebel, Assistant Editor

Trisha Previte, Associate Designer

Ilana Worrell, Senior Production Editor